YOSSEL'S JOURNEY

Kathryn Lasky

Illustrated by Johnson Yazzie

Charlesbridge

For my grandparents Joseph and Ida Lasky, who dared to go west—far west beyond Ellis Island.—K. L.

I dedicate my contribution to this book to my father, Johnson Yazzie, and my mother, Patty R. Yazzie, with gratitude for instilling in me talent and courage. The artistic bloodline of my father's clan made me visible in the eyes of the creator and of his clan. The passion I feel when creating flows in me like the water in a mountain stream. My mother's courage and resiliency provided the shield I use for being a spirited warrior of strength. It is what made this art project possible. My parents would say, "Na'ach'aahigg ei iiyisii boholiih," meaning "art is important." Art is my way of life: a gift from my parents.—J. Y.

Published by Charlesbridge
9 Galen Street
Watertown, MA 02472
(617) 926-0329
www.charlesbridge.com

Library of Congress Cataloging-in-Publication Data
Names: Lasky, Kathryn, author. | Yazzie, Johnson, illustrator.
Title: Yossel's journey / Kathryn Lasky; illustrated by Johnson Yazzie.
Description: Watertown, MA: Charlesbridge Publishing, [2022] | Includes
    bibliographical references. | Audience: Ages 5–9. | Audience: Grades 2–3. |
    Summary: "Yossel, along with his family, flees anti-Jewish Russian pogroms
    in the late nineteenth century and settles in the American Southwest where
    he forges a friendship with Thomas, a Native American Navajo boy."—
    Provided by publisher.
Identifiers: LCCN 2020026145 (print) | LCCN 2020026146 (ebook) |
    ISBN 9781623541767 (hardcover) | ISBN 9781632899675 (ebook)
Subjects: LCSH: Jews—New Mexico—Juvenile fiction. | CYAC: Jews—United
    States—Fiction. | Immigrants—Fiction. | Navajo Indians—Fiction. | Indians
    of North America—New Mexico—Fiction. | Friendship—Fiction. | New
    Mexico—History—19th century—Fiction.
Classification: LCC PZ7.L3274 Yo 2022 (print) | LCC PZ7.L3274 (ebook) |
    DDC [E]—dc23
LC record available at https://lccn.loc.gov/2020026145
LC ebook record available at https://lccn.loc.gov/2020026146

Printed in China
(hc) 10 9 8 7 6 5 4 3 2 1

Illustrations done in acrylic paints on canvas
Display type set in Buffalo by Cruzine
Text type set in Adobe Hebrew by Adobe Systems Incorporated
Color separations by Druidian Archival Service, Phoenix, AZ
Printed by 1010 Printing International Limited in Huizhou, Guangdong, China
Production supervision by Jennifer Most Delaney
Designed by Diane M. Earley

My name is yossel.

This is me telling a funny chicken joke to my best friend, Moishe.

And then this is me saying goodbye to Moishe.

We are going to America because the leader of Russia, the tsar, is sending his soldiers to hurt Jewish people. Mama and Papa have been talking about leaving for a long time. Now they are certain we must go.

No one asks me what I think.

We leave our town, Povpek, at seven-thirty in the morning. I know this because I wear my grandfather's watch. I bring my journal and colored pencils. Mama brings pots, pans, and dried fruit. Papa brings books, tobacco, and our samovar for making tea.

But here is what we cannot bring: our little house that smells like cinnamon and rubs shoulders with our neighbors' houses, the man with the crooked back who gives me a piece of candy for helping him into the synagogue, the lady who sells herring and sings in her smelly little shop, and Moishe.

We take a train to Odessa. From there we take a ship to England, and then we get on another ship headed to New York. We cross the huge Atlantic Ocean.

It takes twelve days, twenty-two hours, and four minutes to get there.

Many people from Russia come here. I eat good food just like what Mama cooked in our town. Here in New York, just like in Povpek, houses rub shoulders, and buildings are so close you can smell what your neighbor is cooking for dinner.

But we are not going to live in New York City. We take a train to the city of Topeka and another train to a town called Santa Fe. But we are not going to a city or a town.

A freight wagon will take us to a place in the desert near a Navajo Indian Reservation. It is called Two Red Hills.

We ride for hours and hours across the huge
land, under the biggest sky I have ever seen.
Sometimes the land stacks up into steep,
flat-topped mountains or rocks called mesas.
They remind me of stone hats.

At last I see a trading post. It is my uncle Isaac's house, where we will live. Before Uncle Izzy died, he sent us money to come to America. Now this house, crouching all by itself under a wide sky in an empty desert, is ours.

Uncle Izzy's trading post is full of things. There are bags of flour, jars of candy and nails, and barrels of coffee and beans and seed. There is rope and soap, hammers and shovels.

Mama tells Papa to fire up the woodstove. Soon I smell the same thing I smelled ten thousand miles ago in Povpek—cinnamon!

Now Mama is making her honey cake for a special Sabbath dessert. I help drop the bits of candied fruit into the batter. I love to discover them buried like treasure in the middle of the cake.

Just before the sun sets, Mama lights the Sabbath candles and says the Hebrew blessing. I imagine the words spinning off into the sky. I look out the window toward the mesas. Their shadows turn purple and stretch across the land. The smell of sagebrush meets the cinnamon of Mama's honey cake. I breathe it all in.

People begin to come to the store. Sometimes cowboys, but most of our visitors are Navajo Indians. The women bring rugs they have woven for Mama to weigh and sell. They bargain, talking with their hands as much as their mouths. Mama has good, long talking fingers!

Sometimes the women come with children. When they do, I hide, but I always listen. I learn English and Navajo words for things like coffee and nails. I learn scolding words for when their babies are naughty. But I am afraid to speak.

Today an old Navajo woman comes in to trade. She has a baby in a cradleboard on her back and a boy by her side.

"How old?" Mama asks.

"Baby three months. Boy is eight," the woman says. "My grandchildren."

"My Yossel is eight," Mama says. She smiles and looks for me, but I am hiding.

I want to speak to this boy, but the words fly away like birds. Then I hear a funny, gurgly sound: *Baa!*

It's not English. It's not Navajo. It's not Yiddish.

It's sheep!

I see the whitest, wooliest sheep prancing like a whirling blizzard through the trading post.

I jump out from behind the barrel. "Stop, sheep!" I shout—in English!

Finally we catch that blizzard and tie her up outside.

"Name?" I ask, pointing at the sheep.

"Sooh'bii'naah'. Star Eye," the boy says, tracing the starry black patch around her eye with his finger.

He points to himself. "Thomas," he says. Then he adds "Good dii'beeh', good sheep." *Dibeh.*

Mama calls. "Come, boys, have tea."

Mama has put glasses of hot tea on the table. I reach for
a lump of sugar and put it in my mouth. Thomas stares.

"In Russia, like this." Mama puts the sugar in her mouth
and takes a swallow of tea.

Thomas does this, too. He smiles.

Then Mama puts hot blintzes on a plate.

"*Mmmmmmm!*" Thomas says, taking a big bite.

I laugh. Thomas *really* likes blintzes!

The next day Thomas comes back. We drink tea, eat blintzes, and play with Star Eye. Then I decide to tell my chicken joke. I try to find the right words, but when I finish, he just looks confused.

After Thomas leaves, I think about Moishe, who *always* laughed at my jokes. Then I think of the herring lady and the man with the crooked back.

Here, there is mostly silence. Here, there is mostly nothing at all.

One day Thomas returns. I try to make everything perfect: no jokes; lots of blintzes. But then something happens. While we are eating, Star Eye eats something, too—a big hole in my father's underwear!

"Oy!" Mama shouts. You don't have to know Yiddish to know she is angry.

"Mama! Mama! Stop!" I shout. My mama is chasing away my new friend's sheep!

Star Eye leaps a fence, and Thomas scrambles after her. I watch as they disappear.

I go to my bed. My one chance for a friend in America—ruined!

The next day there is no Thomas. He does not come the day after that or even the next.

Then one day I am in the back room when I hear a snort. "Star Eye!" The sheep is peeking in my window! I hug her and kiss her, and then I see Thomas crouching by the wall and smiling. I crawl out the window. He looks the same. He smiles and says one word. "Blintzes."

Mama comes out just then. "Blintzes," she agrees.
"Bring sheep in. Better she eat blintzes than underwear!"
Everyone laughs, even Thomas. Mama has made a joke!

Thomas comes the next day, too, and many days after that. He shows me where the ghosts of Navajos live and where rattlesnakes sleep.

One day Thomas announces, "I'll take you to a town."
I look around. "No town—just sky and mountains!"
But Thomas insists. "Yes, a town."
"A real town?" It's hard to believe.

We take leftover blintzes and walk for a long, long time.

Finally Thomas stops. Then he points.

All I see are humps of dirt. *Some town!* I think.

"Wait," says Thomas.

He whistles softly. Suddenly a furry little snout pokes out of a hump. Then another and another! Thomas starts laughing.

"What's this?" I ask.

Thomas is laughing so hard he can hardly speak. "Prairie dog town."

I start laughing, too.

That evening Thomas invites me to spend the night
at his hogan. A hogan is a Navajo house made of logs
and mud. Mama hands me a sack with gifts for
Thomas's family.

Where Thomas lives, there is not just one hogan.
There are two—Thomas's and his auntie's. The hogans
almost touch shoulders, just like in Povpek.

Inside Thomas's house, I meet his mother, father,
and older sister. There are no windows here, but I
can see the sky through the opening in the roof. For
supper there is chicken stew. I take a bite and think
of my chicken joke. But should I tell it?

Then Thomas's mother asks, "You like this chicken?"
I take a deep breath and say, "Yes, but I have a question."
Everyone is looking at me now. Even the baby.

All right, I think.
"Chicken soup. Is it good for your health?"
Thomas's parents nod.
Then I pick up a piece of chicken and wave it in
the air. "Not if you're the chicken!"
There is only silence.

But then the baby picks up his spoon and waves it in the air and gurgles. Suddenly, everyone seems to get the joke.

"If you're the chicken, you're dead!" Thomas shouts. And now everyone is laughing. The baby begins to laugh!

And then the family starts pointing at the baby. They yell. They whoop.

"First laugh out loud!" Thomas keeps saying. He is trying hard to explain.

Finally I understand. When a baby laughs out loud for the first time, Navajos celebrate. They will have a party. Because I made the baby laugh, I will have a special role.

When it is time for bed, I unroll my blanket near
Thomas. His mother puts a thick woolly sheep fleece on
the ground for us to sleep on.

Thomas shows me a chink in the wall, and I can see
the moon rising over a stone hat. I think of the baby's first
laugh and how I was the one who made that baby laugh.

I am cozy. I am warm. The land does not look so empty,
and the sky does not look so big. The stars come closer,
and nothing is silent. I laugh out loud into the night.

My name is Yossel.
This is my house in the desert.
This is my friend Thomas.
We live in America.

AUTHOR'S NOTE

I've always been interested in Jewish immigrants who did not settle, as so many others did, on the Lower East Side of New York when they arrived in the late nineteenth century. My own Jewish grandparents came in through Halifax, Nova Scotia, and settled in Duluth, Minnesota. A few Jewish families made their way much farther and operated trading posts in the Southwest, like Yossel's family does. The Danoff brothers, for example, were Jewish pioneers who settled in Gallup, New Mexico. They began a trading post that Native people called the Honest Man Trading Post. Another pair of brothers, Solomon and Simon Bibo, settled near Acoma Pueblo in New Mexico and opened a trading business. Many of their customers were Navajo or Pueblo people.

Jewish roots in the American Southwest go back much further than the nineteenth century. In the fifteenth century, Jews were expelled from Spain during the Spanish Inquisition, and many sought refuge in the part of Mexico that eventually became the state of New Mexico. Forced to conceal their religion, they were often known as Marranos, Conversos, or even crypto-Jews ("secret Jews"). After generations of spiritual subterfuge and repression, many of them gradually lost their heritage and became practicing Catholics. Yet they still clung to customs such as lighting candles on Friday night, not eating pork, and never mixing meat and dairy products. Over generations, these Jews began to intermarry with people of both Spanish and Native American descent.

My novel *Blood Secret* tells the story of these secret Jews. While researching that book, I traveled to New Mexico several times and on more than one occasion came across cemeteries with headstones that were carved with both crosses and Jewish Stars of David. There I learned of Navajo and Pueblo people who, upon discovering their Jewish roots, decided to study Hebrew so they could celebrate their bar mitzvahs and bat mitzvahs, even though they were well past the age of thirteen. I found all this to be an unbelievably rich history. Although Yossel, Thomas, Povpek, and Two Red Hills are fictional, I'm sure that once upon a time there was a Navajo boy and an immigrant Jewish boy who became best friends in the far west of this country. I wanted to celebrate that friendship in this story. Part of being a writer is believing that a story that begins in your imagination could possibly happen—and then breathing life into it.

FURTHER READING

Lasky, Kathryn. *Marven of the Great North Woods*. Boston: Houghton Mifflin, 1997.

A true story based on the experiences of the author's father, Marven Lasky. As the 1918 flu epidemic sweeps the nation, Marven's parents fear for their son's life and send Marven to a logging camp in the North Woods of Minnesota to escape the epidemic. A National Jewish Book Award winner.

Lasky, Kathryn. *The Night Journey*. New York: Frederick Warne, 1981.

Rachel learns about her great-grandmother Nana Sashie's childhood experience of the pogroms in Russia in this story, which is loosely based on the escape of the author's aunt from tsarist Russia. A National Jewish Book Award winner.

Marks, M. L. *Jews Among the Indians: Tales of Adventure and Conflict in the Old West*. Chicago: Benison Books, 1995.

A fascinating story of the American frontier, when Jewish and Native American people first encountered one another. An adventure with unexpected heroism and unforgettable characters.

Rochlin, Harriet and Fred. *Pioneer Jews: A New Life in the Far West*. Boston: Houghton Mifflin, 1984.

An illustrated social history of a not-often-told story about the Jewish experience beyond Ellis Island and New York. Filled with colorful anecdotes.

Tobias, Henry J. A. *A History of the Jews in New Mexico*. Albuquerque: University of New Mexico Press, 1990, 1992.

One of the first histories of Jewish life in New Mexico, the book traces the colonial experience through the present day. It covers the crypto-Jews who came north from Mexico to escape the Mexican Inquisition, as well as the German Jewish merchants who found their way to Las Vegas, Santa Fe, and other cities after railroads were built in the nineteenth century. A thorough account of the origins of Jewish development in New Mexico.